The Christmas Star

By Marcus Pfister

Translated by J. Alison James

North-South Books

NEW YORK

The night the three shepherds were visited by angels, even their sheep were agitated. The shepherds gathered around the campfire talking in excited voices:

"An infant King, without Lords or Knights . . ."

"But strong!"

"Stronger than any King has ever been."

"And yet kind and merciful. A King of peace and joy!"

Books by Marcus Pfister

The Rainbow Fish*
Rainbow Fish to the Rescue!*
The Christmas Star*
Dazzle the Dinosaur*
I See the Moon
Milo and the Magical Stones*
Penguin Pete*
Penguin Pete's New Friends*
Penguin Pete and Pat
Penguin Pete and Little Tim
Penguin Pete, Ahoy!
Hopper*
Hopper Hunts for Spring
Hopper's Easter Surprise
Hang On, Hopper!
Hopper's Treetop Adventure
Wake Up, Santa Claus!

*also available in Spanish

First mini-hardcover edition published in 1997 by North-South Books.
Copyright © 1993 by Nord-Süd Verlag AG, Gossau Zürich, Switzerland
First published in Switzerland under the title Der Weihnachtstern
English translation copyright © 1993 by North-South Books Inc.

First published in the United States, Great Britain, Canada,
Australia, and New Zealand in 1997 by North-South Books,
an imprint of Nord-Süd Verlag AG, Gossau Zürich, Switzerland.

Distributed in the United States by North-South Books Inc., New York.

Library of Congress Cataloging-in-Publication Data is available.
A CIP catalogue record for this book is available
from The British Library.

ISBN 1-55858-822-1
1 3 5 7 9 10 8 6 4 2
Printed in Italy

"Let us go down to Bethlehem to see this newborn King," suggested the oldest shepherd.

"But how shall we find Him? All we know is that He is wrapped in swaddling clothes and lying in a manger."

"If only we could fly above the city and look into all the houses, like the eyes of the stars. Surely these stars know the place of the Holy Child's birth!"

The three shepherds were looking up at the sky when suddenly the stars began to move!

Slowly they flowed toward one another, closer and closer, until finally they merged into a single magnificent star. This star with its shining tail swept a radiant glow across the deep blue night.

Then the star slowly dipped toward the horizon. Hastily the shepherds packed up their belongings. They gathered the sheep together and followed the mysterious star. It was guiding them to Bethlehem, to see the Holy Child.

There was a King who lived in a splendid palace in the East. That very night he saw the star and remembered a prophecy of old. It was said there would be a King of Kings, a Lord of Lords, a Prince of Peace. After many painful years of war, he and his people longed for a time of harmony among nations.

From the great balcony the King and his attendants watched the star. Its shining light reflected like the sun off the golden domes of his palace.

"This Child has come to show us the way to peace," said the King. "I will go and bid Him welcome. The bright star in the heavens will guide me."

*So the King rode forth from his palace bearing precious
gifts for the young Prince.*

That same night he met two other Kings who were following the star. He spoke to them: "Let us go together to the Prince of Peace. Let us give Him our gifts, our faith, and our love."

So the three Kings journeyed through the desert toward Bethlehem.

The brilliant light of the star penetrated even the darkness of the deep forest.

"It must be the full moon," thought the wolf, and he began to howl.

But when the light grew stronger, the curious animals ran to the edge of the woods and looked up at the sky.

The owl was waiting and gave them the news. "A Child has been born," she told them. "A Holy Child who will love and care for all living things. The bright light in the sky is a glorious star, calling us all to Bethlehem."

Drawn by the light, the animals went fearlessly on their way.

The star finally came to rest over a tiny stable, bathing it in clear light.

Everyone wanted to welcome the Child and celebrate the spirit of harmony that had brought them together. So the mountain lion lay down among the sheep, and the fox lay down by the hare, and the powerful Kings from the East talked like brothers with the humble shepherds.

Quiet and peace nestled over the land like a blanket. Inside the stable, the Holy Child fell asleep, and the glorious Christmas Star blazed its beacon of hope over all.